Seven Deadly Sins of a Pirate

Smew's Greed   Volume One: Part 1

Younger pirates can check

Smew's Nook

on YouTube for popular pirate stories read by Captain Smew.

More videos coming soon!

https://www.youtube.com/watch?v=cfUguz6r78I

Coming soon
Free Audio Book Version of Smew's Greed:
Author Web page:

https://www.RichardWDyer.com

Seven Deadly Sins of a Pirate:

Smew's Greed

Volume One: Part I

Richard W. Dyer

Smew Publishing

TO MY FATHER
Who inspired me with a love of books
at a very young age

See the Book Trailer Here: https://www.youtube.com/watch?v=UfHGseZULx8
Instagram: @busboat_pirate
Crowd Funding Efforts: https://www.gofundme.com/9b8589x3
Author Web page: https://www.RichardWDyer.com
Facebook: https://www.facebook.com/captain.saif.t.smew.pyrate/?ref=hl

Chapter One
Wet Arrival

"Swim Shiva! Swim! Harder! Swim little tadpole. You can do this! I know you can." Captain Smew encouraged the little pirate, who by now was exhausted beyond all comprehension. She had a cramp in her left leg, her arms ached like crazy and they were so weak she could barely move them to tread water, let alone to swim.

Shiva wasn't a very strong swimmer to begin with, but fighting this current was brutal. Her sword and baldric weighed heavy across her shoulder but to Shiva's credit, she refused to toss them aside. Smew quickly looked around to assess their situation.

Amadahy and Candelario were just on the other side of the breaking waves. They would soon be safe on land. Good. Amadahy, the best swimmer of them all, was nearly to shore. Candelario had just made it through the pounding surf.

Smew told the other two to get to shore so Amadahy could help Candelario, who was a mediocre swimmer at best, while he stayed behind to help Shiva.

"I'm jus' too tired Capitan." Shiva's eyes begged for deliverance from the pain and fatigue that wracked her little body.   "Shiva, Jus' grab hold o' me shirt. Can ye at least do that, love?"

"Aye Cap'n. I'll try," she replied feebly. Smew struggled to get Shiva to fight. Grabbing her by the shoulders, he shook her once to snap her out of her fatigued state and wake her up.

"Shiva! Ye must swim! Yer life depends on it!" he cried, emphasizing the word 'life' as he pleaded with her to keep fighting.

The swells were lifting them up and dropping them down. The water was turquoise blue and still too deep to see the ocean floor. While in the bottom of the trough, water towering above them was all they could see. They did not seem to be advancing much. Smew was just beginning to realize they were caught in a riptide. He wasn't the greatest swimmer either, but he was strong and determined to not let Shiva drown. When he put his mind to something there was no changing it. "Shiva, we have to swim that way," he ordered, pointing parallel to shore.

"But the beach is that way," a bewildered Shiva protested, looking straight at the beach she pointed with her little nose because her hands were busy treading water.

"Riptide," was Smew's reply as Shiva's eyes widened in fear. Her eyes darted, her breathing quickened and panic threatened to strangle all reason.

Smew gently cupped Shiva's face in his hands. He locked his eyes to hers, he took a deep breath and then another, causing a reflex response in her. In a moment her breathing matched his. "It's alright, love. We'll get through this," Smew reassured her. "Jus' grab hold and don't let go—and kick like yer life depends on it! I'll do the rest." Smew began to swim diagonally toward the beach, not fighting the rip. It was working. After several minutes, instead of being in the bottom of the trough they were starting to come up on top. Fighting to crawl their way out of the trough and up the back of each wave was like sliding through shale. It seemed that for every two feet gained they lost one.

He could feel the weight of his boots, sword, pistol, and Shiva all dragging against him. His limbs burned with fire. Never could he remember his body being wracked with more pain than this. As much perhaps, but not more. But it *was* working. They were slowly inching closer to shore. "Okay Shiva, now we gonna be havin' to swim real hard to catch the next wave. Can you do that, love?"

Shiva nodded, gasping for breath and unable to speak. It was all she could do to hold onto the bottom of Smew's thick black shirt. As he swam, he kept kicking her in the ribs; not all the time but enough to hurt. As the wave built behind them Captain Smew signaled, "Now! Swim hard, lil' tadpole!" He called her that since the first day he saw her, because she was so tiny and she reminded him of a baby frog with so much energy.

They both started kicking. Smew felt the push of the wave behind him as he swam with nearly every ounce of strength he had left. Finally they would be safe. He rode the wave for all it was worth, until it crashed on top of him and rolled him over and over under the water.

It be hard to tell which way is up when ye be getting' churned like butter, he thought. He finally got his head above the water and took a much needed breath. "Shiva!" he yelled. He didn't feel her pulling on him. Frantically he searched the chest deep water around him for any sign of her. *She must still be under this frothy sea,* he thought, as he thrashed the water with his hands and feet to feel for her.

"Shiva!" He screamed again. He struggled to fight back the fear that clawed at the edges of his mind. *Even the thought that I could lose her..,* he thought.

Just then he heard Candelario and Amadahy who were running down the beach and screaming from shore. They were pointing out to sea.

He looked around wildly for his little tadpole and to his shock and horror saw that she had not made the last wave. She was more than 100 feet behind the breaks. Her arms were up in the air as if reaching for a rope or outstretched hand. With head tilted back, her face was barely out of the water. "Shiva! I'm coming," he yelled, as he started swimming with everything he had. *Harder Smew. You got to get to her,* his muscles screamed with every stroke to stop.

Something drove him on, despite the pain. *I have to save her. I have to.* It was agonizing to see her struggle to keep her head above water. Poor thing, Smew thought. *Hang on Little Tadpole. Capitan Smew gunna save ye, love, or die tryin'!*

5

Smew was several feet from Shiva when her head and arms sank below the surface and out of sight. *Were that the second or third time she be goin' under?* Captain Smew wondered. He understood the third time meant a person was drowning. Bending at the waist and raising his feet into the air to propel him downward, he dove beneath the surface. Her limp body slowly sank toward the cold dark-blue water below. Smew grabbed her tiny hands, then walked his hands down her arms to her body, all the while lifting her toward the surface, and air.

Once at the surface, Smew shook her awake. Her dark brown eyes were rolled back in her head, her face was blueish, she had given up and was barely conscious. He yelled in her face, "Shiva! Wake up Shiva!"

Shiva blinked, slowly at first, as if awakening from a deep drug induced stupor. She fought to roll her eyes back to where she could see who held her, and who was screaming. *Cap'n Smew,* she thought. You *came back.* "I can't," was all she said. Her little body went limp in his hands.

"Shiva nooooo!" Smew was not going to let her give up. He knew he could not tow her to shore without her help, so unless she helped they would both drown because he would not leave her there.

In desperation, Smew raised his hand and slapped her on the cheek, hard. His emotions got the better of him though, and the slap carried more force than he intended.

Shiva opened her brown crescent eyes but this time there was fire there.

"SCALLAWAG!" she blurted in anger.

7

"Do I need to do that again or will ye swim?" Smew was ready to slap her with hand outstretched.

"No, nnno, I'll swim," Shiva replied. "But... I'm... so tired," she whispered.

"I know, love, but we can do this," Smew reassured her. "You just have to hang onto me. I won't let you drown. I not gonna leave ye, love. I promise.

"Your shirt pulled out before. What if I can't hold on again?"

"Wait, gimme that rope," he demanded. Shiva always carried a rope over her shoulder. She liked tying knots and she always said, "It jus' might come in handy someday, ye know." She was too tired to remove it so Smew took it off her while she struggled to tread water and stay afloat.

Like now, Smew thought to himself. *Jus' how handy ye never knew, tadpole.* Smew hastily tied a bowline around Shiva and one around himself. He told her to grab the rope around his waist and hang on, and kick. She promised she would. One good kick in her bruised ribs and Shiva let some rope slide through her hands to put a little distance between herself and those boots.

Again they were in position to swim for a wave. It flattened and passed them by. "It's okay, we gonna be gettin' the next one," Smew told her.

The two exhausted pirates treaded water, waiting for the next wave. "Here it comes, now swim! Swim, kick, kick, kick!"

9

Shiva seemed too exhausted to fight the waves that kept smashing into her, making it impossible for her to catch her breath or get her balance. Like driftwood she bobbed along. Each wave slammed her as it arrived then pulled on her as it left. She had no more gumption than a piece of seaweed long since torn from its roots. Exhausted she lie mostly face down in the water.

After what seemed like forever, Smew finally untangled the rope from around his feet and quickly found Shiva. She was at the end of her rope, unable to stand up. Captain Smew scooped her up in his powerful arms. With his back to the sea Smew struggled to get to his feet. It was all he could do to stand with Shiva. Her dead weight combined with the action of the approaching wave that sucked them both back toward the sea, which then crashed on top of them, the sand constantly shifting beneath his feet.

Again he tried to stand but was slammed in the back by a wall of water. He did his best to protect the listless girl in his arms. They both went down hard with Smew on top of her. His focus was split between trying to stand and keeping Shiva's face out of the water. Again he struggled to erect himself against the shifting sand and the powerful waves that kept hitting them both and sucking them back out to sea. Something new seemed to be wrapped around Smew's legs, or feet, because he could not get them to move where he wanted them to go.

Is it that darned rope again, our baldrics, or my sash that keeps tying up my feet? With one hand around Shiva's leg and another around her torso Smew was not able to tell, but between the waves, Shiva's languid body, and his waterlogged clothes and boots, it was infuriating not being able to get to his feet. *I need to get Shiva out on dry land and I surely don't want us getting chewed up any more on that coral,* he thought.

A frustrated Smew yelled at Amadahy and Candelario, who had run down the beach, by this time, and were coming out to help. "What arrr ye waiting for? Give us a hand will ye?"

Another wave knocked Smew down as he struggled to regain his balance. It also took out Candelario. Candelario began to be sucked out to the sharp rocks and jagged coral but regained footing enough to finally stand and provide some aid. Amadahy didn't seem too sure of what to do. Her well-worn boots fell down around her ankles and she could hardly walk in the shifting sand. She stayed back, apparently not wanting to suffer the same fate as Candelario, so she waited for a more opportune time to jump in.

Chapter Two
Pyrate vs. Nature

19

$\mathcal{L}$ike refugee rats escaping a sinking ship the four water-logged pirates finally stumbled to shore only to collapse on the beach. It wasn't pretty, but it was at least safe from the tumultuous wave action of moments earlier. But now they had a bigger problem.

Shiva wasn't breathing. Smew slapped her on the back several times but she did not respond. He spun her like a rag doll, wrapped both of his hands around her belly and pulled, several times. He pulled in and upwards. *I gotta get the water out of her stomach and lungs, make her lungs begin to breathe again,* he thought. On the third gut compression, Shiva coughed, then she projectile vomited copious amounts of seawater and began taking in deep breaths of life giving air, followed by more coughing.

After a minute, Shiva looked up at Captain Smew and mustered a weak smile. Then she rested her tired head on his shoulder. Exhausted the four friends sat on the beach, too tired to speak but grateful for every breath of air that entered their lungs.

"Where did ye learn that trick?" Candelario asked.

"I just knew it," was all he replied.

"Well, you just saved her life. We owe you her life."

"Balderdash. That's jus' what family does," Smew replied, grateful that it worked.

Smew stood first. Realizing how close to death they had all just come, especially Shiva, the anger started down in his gut. Deep inside, his blood felt as if it were water just starting to boil. The steam rose to the surface of his flushed face. A bubble of bile erupted in his stomach. The gas it produced left a bitter acidic taste in a mouth already salty from his recent swim to shore.

Through sandy gritted teeth he muttered, "Me own treacherous, cargo thievin' crew marooned us here on this uncharted rock betwixt and between charted waters, with nary a wee bit o' grub! A mutiny? And now we be marooned on this God-forsaken chunk of rock".

"Aye Cap'n", Candelario interrupted his thoughts, "Had our luck been better, our spoils not so sparse…" Candelario's voice trailed off. He noted his first mate's attempt to soothe his anger, and wondered if the comment was stopped when Candelario realized how badly the truth of it stung. It mattered little at this point.

Smew's attention was fixed on the Amazing Grace as she sailed toward the horizon. The afternoon sun cast its yellow-orange light across the sea, the rolling surf bringing in the tide. The waves of earlier had gone, leaving a flat sea in their stead.

Then, suddenly, the captain spotted an unmistakable shape wallowing in the froth.

Ahoy tharr, ye lice infested, skirt wearin', parrot lovin', landlubber scallywags! Fer the duration of this here volume, I gonna be yer narrator. Now, contrary to what ye landlubbers may be thinkin' o' them scurvy pyrates, generally speakin', their lootin' an' plunderin', even the takin' o' prisoners, were all sometimes guided by a set of ethics: a pyrate's code if ye will. Fer instance, when mutineering pyrates were forced to maroon one o' their own, they tended to leave the marooned pyrate, or pyrates, as be the case with Smew and his little crew, with provisions—enough rum, saltbacon, citris fruits (prevents the scurvy, don't ye know), and other such commodities, and in this way the mutineers could 'ave a legal leg to stand on if accused o' murder later on.

However, conditions on Smew's ship had been abysmal, and there wasn't much food to spare. In addition to a wee bit o' moldy bread, Smew and his companions were allowed one bottle of rum and their weapons, which it were also customary fer the one doing the marooning to allow the one bein' marooned, jus' in case the marooned pyrate decided t' take his own life in a moment o' despair.

Avast ye! Now git back to yer story, ye lice infested, parrot lovin' swabs!

"Avast ye thar, me hearties! Th' sea's returned me trusty tricorn! Yah harrrr!" Exhausted limbs found new strength as Smew clamored and sloshed down the beach to retrieve his three cornered leather hat. He emptied it of seawater, and pompously placed it upon his head. It felt proper to be wearing the emblem of his authority, even if his ship had just been stolen.

Still, neither the wind on his face, nor the smell of the thick salty air in his nostrils could overcome the fact that he was standing in water-logged boots on a sandy beach instead of where he should be. His short-lived elation was quickly replaced with ire as he squinted through bloodshot eyes at the tiny spec of a ship, his ship, shrinking on the horizon.

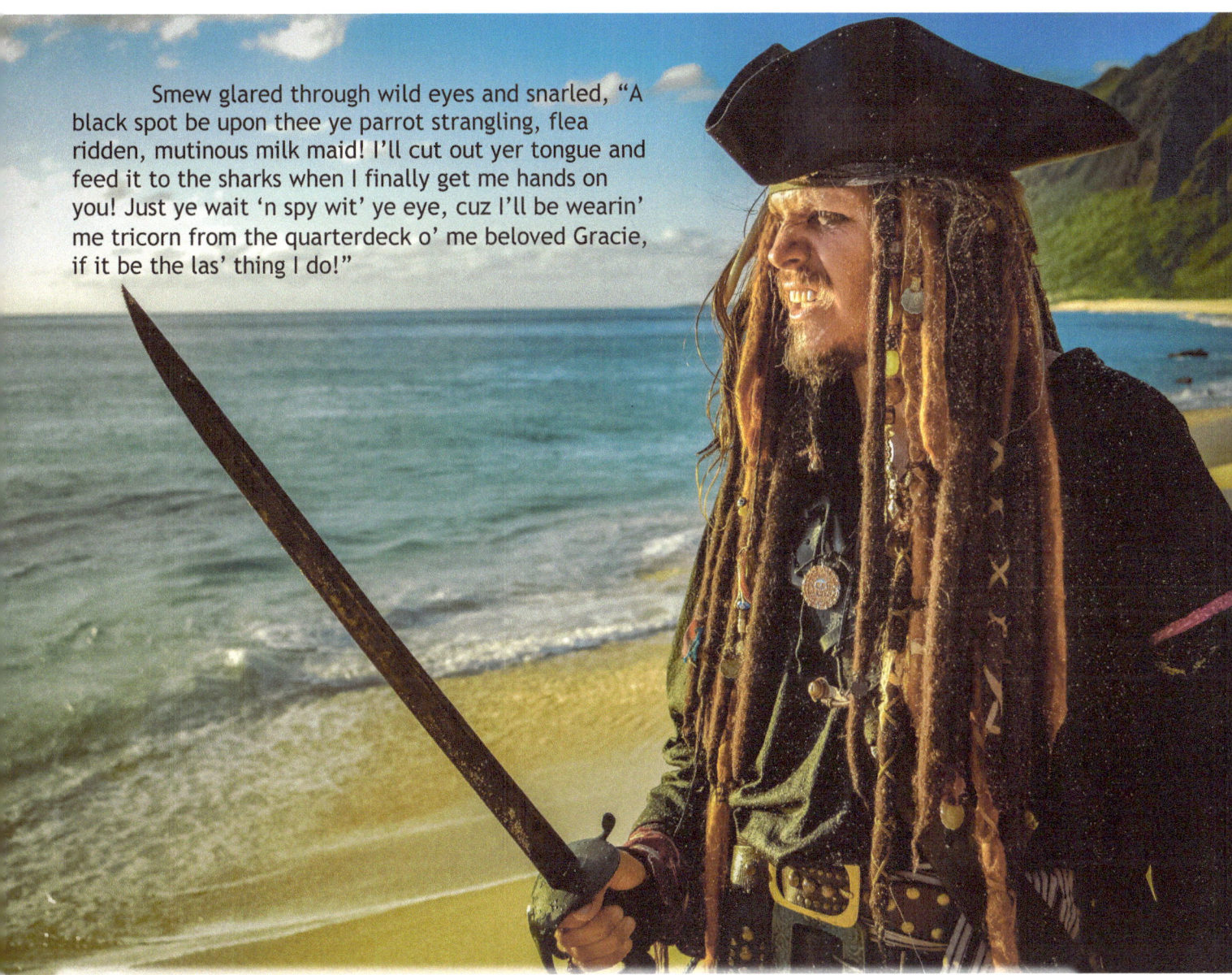

Smew glared through wild eyes and snarled, "A black spot be upon thee ye parrot strangling, flea ridden, mutinous milk maid! I'll cut out yer tongue and feed it to the sharks when I finally get me hands on you! Just ye wait 'n spy wit' ye eye, cuz I'll be wearin' me tricorn from the quarterdeck o' me beloved Gracie, if it be the las' thing I do!"

With that he spat on the beach, sword drawn and fist clenched. In spite of this bravado, Smew knew they weren't coming back. He was here for good. His revenge must wait. But at least he knew who his friends were. Three loyal mates who were still sprawled on the beach regaining their strength. He knew they could be trusted and that knowledge gave him some peace. They had saved each others' lives more times than he could remember. *Focus Smew. They be needin' ye to be strong, not to fall apart like that rot-stricken, roach infested rowboat,* he told himself while staring out to sea.

A gentle tug on his elbow brought him back. Smew had long ago ceased to be startled by Amadahy's ability to appear at his side, as if from thin air. She pulled him sideways until her mouth nearly touched his ear. "Avast ye tharr yon sea creature, Capt'n," her warm breath permeated his dreads and found its mark. Pointing down the beach, "If ye shoot, Amadahy cook. What say ye Capt'n?" Just then he heard her stomach rumble.

"Well, shave me belly with a wench's tonails!" exclaimed Smew as he rubbed the warm moist air from his ear. It tickled when Amadahy whispered like that. In fact, it made the hair on the back of his neck stand up and gave him goose bumps on that half of his body. "We best not upset th' balance o' thin's by killin' such a placid creature. If yer hungry, I'll hunt fer more fittin' grub."

"Well Capt'n, it were many weeks since our last meal of meat," Amadahy said. "Through no fault of the Capt'n'".

Just then, Smew's keen eye spotted movement off in the distance. It was some fowl scratching in the dirt at the edge of the grass. "I'd settle fer some cackle-fruit, but them wee birdies might make fer fine eatin'," he whispered, as he left the immediate presence of his companions to stalk his prey. In the brush it was hard to line up a clean shot. He tracked the birds and waited for the right moment. When he was within 20 yards and could see no branches in the way, he took aim with his flintlock pistol, pulled the trigger, and...tink! The hammer hit the flash-pan, but nothing happened.

The skittish birds, hearing the sound, clucked and crashed off into the bushes. "Scurvy flea bitten bilge rats", he grumbled, cursing his boatswain and master gunner.

They were two main conspirators who led the mutiny on board his ship. It was they who had thrown his pistols to him in a fishnet bag on the end of a rope, ensuring the powder was too wet to fire back at them. Their mocking laughter rang in his ears. His own helplessness in the face of their betrayal made his rage swell up all over again.

He took some deep breaths. Smew calmly, slowly bent over and picked up a rock, roughly the size of his fist. *It be th' possession of a magical spyglass wot be givin' a certain pirate captain th' upper hand when it comes to searchin' fer things wot be worth searchin' for*, he thought.

Smew took a knee, cleared his mind, and focused on finding those fat spotted fowl. The spyglass showed 3 of them hiding behind a large rock enshrouded by bushes with yellow flowers. He lowered the tiny abalone shell covered brass telescope, located the bush and from down wind, he snuck around behind it. When he had a clear shot Smew threw that rock as hard as he could at the closest bird's head.

A clean shot dispatched the speckled bird in its tracks. The fowl's companions clucked and fluttered off into the bushes. *We not gonna be goin' hungry tonight*, thought the captain. "Be ye famished, Candy-boy?" Captain Smew turned and called to his mate. He hadn't realized how far into the grass he tracked his game.

Avast ye tharr, ye rotten timbered, barnacle bottomed scabby sea bass! Me thinks it be high time ye knowed 'bout a certain spyglass wot be danglin' 'round the cap'n's neck. The way she werks is the one wot holds her must concentrate on wot they seek. Wot he were performin' some bad deed that day then the little magical telescope won't be doing ye no favors, thas fer sure.

Cap'n Smew were fortunate enuff to have jus' such a magical spyglass, a tiny abalone shell-covered brass telescope that normally only magnifies about double power. So far, in our story, Smew ain't done nothin' too incredibly mean or cruel to anyone, at least not today, and in fact earned the rewards of th' glass by rescuin' little Shiva. Keep a weather eye out for it, me hearties!

None of them were in sight, but Smew knew what they would be about. Surely Candelario had gone to look for a safe place to camp. Smew's first mate would be gathering firewood that would provide warmth and protection against the night and he would likely send Amadahy and Shiva to forage something for their dinner. Smew knew this because this was not the first time they had made camp on land.

Smew wondered if Shiva would find a nice warm place to take a nap, which was something she loved to do. It had been an exhausting day, what with being thrown off their ship into a rickety skiff, rowing to shore, only to have the skiff break up in the surf, and finally having to swim to shore, the riptide of course, and nearly drowning in the process. Yes, Captain Smew was sure it had taken it's toll on the young lass. Hardened as she was from this life, he knew she was still a child at heart.

As it turned out, she found a nice warm rock to lie down on while Candelario and Amadahy went to forage something to eat for dinner.

Knowing they would need sticks on which to cook the meat, Smew found a bush that had green branches the thickness of his thumb. "That will do the job jus' fine," he mused. He bent over to make the cut, but when he stood back up his hair was tangled in kiawe bush. The kiawe tree has thorns that will easily pierce a well-worn boot.

"Well skewer me worm infested gizzard," he muttered under his breath. "These blasted thorns! 'Tis as if they be tryin' to snatch me bald headed! When I git out of here I'll remember this bush to make me some fish hooks," he said. It seemed the more Smew struggled to free himself from the 2 inch long thorns, the more his dreads and his shirt became entangled.

Chapter Three
Curses

Taking care not to tear his shirt, he removed his knife from the sheath in his upper belt and began to cut away at the thorny hard wood bush that kept him trapped. *I have actually seen little birds skewered by these noxious weeds,* he thought. Piece by painstaking piece, Smew untangled his hair from the kiawe bush into which he had stumbled. In spite of his grumbling, Smew managed to make it to camp with his hair intact. What he saw when he arrived there made him proud, but for some reason he could not bring himself to compliment his crew.

Amadahy was having Shiva help her prepare the food and Candelario was whittling on a stick as Captain Smew walked into the camp area. "Don't be swinging the lead mate", the captain reminded, "and we'll be needin' more than a wee bit o' shavin's to get th' fire started, savvy?" Candelario was intrigued by Smew's knack for telling people what they must surely already know.

"Aye aye, Cap'n! More than a wee bit it is," replied Candelario, with a slight shake of his head and a little grin.

Shiva who had taken a much needed nap at Candelario's insistence, came over to see what the captain had brought for meat. Smew handed the birds to Amadahy for her to clean and ready the fowl for cooking. The captain prepared to ignite the fire by first gathering Candelario's shavings, his own kindling, and tinder he made from some dry bark. Striking a piece of flint with the back of Amadahy's knife produced sparks. But one hasty and misplaced strike produced sharp pain when Smew hit the tip of his thumb with the back of the knife.

"Arrrgh!!" muttered the captain.

"Are you alright Capitán?" Shiva asked, rushing to aid her wounded captain.

"Meeeh, It weren't bad" assured Smew, dismissing her concern cavalierly, not wanting to seem like a baby, though his thumb was throbbing. With flint and steel, he finally got the pile to smoke. Blowing on it produced a flame on which he gently added Candelario's whittlings and the split branches.

Shiva, seeing the flames began smiling and wanted to help pile on the wood. "Too much and it gonna go out", he told her when it was still struggling. They carefully positioned the wood in a criss-cross pattern to keep from smothering the little fire. "Me thumb be bleeding a wee bit," he remarked matter of factly. He stuck it in his mouth to clean it off with his tongue and spit the dirt and blood next to the fire. Shiva pulled the corners of her eyes and mouth down, sniffed a couple of times and turning her bottom lip inside out, made a crybaby face that made Smew laugh. Then they both laughed.

The captain was still adding kindling so the coals would build up quickly, lecturing his crew as he did so of fire building guidelines that dictate that smaller diameter wood burns faster than bigger logs. Again Smew reminded them of something they knew all too well: "Not until th' fire burns down gunna be th' hour to put th' day's kill on a stick, 'n cook it o'er the red steamin' coals."

"Tend ye to the fire, Tadpole, as I be off to see a man about a horse," said the captain, as he walked off into the bushes.

43

Although the fire needed no more shavings, Candelario, lost in thought, stared blankly through the flames and whittled, aware, yet indifferent to the popping firebrands erupting in front of him. Staring into the fire had transported Candelario's troubled mind to another place, long ago.

Candelario remembered the smoke filled room, and the lifeless, blood-soaked bodies of the royal family. Princess Shiva, lying in a puddle of blood, still breathing, her tiny arm bleeding even as Candelario scooped her up and ran out of the palace into the woods to escape the rebel army.

How would the now stranded first mate be able to accumulate enough treasure to buy an army and restore the princess to her castle? *The emperor.* Candelario wondered if he was even still alive. *After all, it has been ten years*, Candelario thought. *No, I cannot allow meself such thoughts. Emperor Chong Zhen must surely still be alive.*

After years of running and hiding, they had finally taken in with Captain Saif T. Smew. Normally Candelario kept a low profile but that was definitely not a fair fight.

Three against one. As gratitude for Candelario's aid, Smew had offered a position on board his vessel, and he promised riches. Candelario shook off the troubling thoughts and returned to the present. Riches indeed. Now they were here, trapped on this island.

Where are we? Candelario wondered, having no clue where they were; none of them did, for this island was not on any charts they had ever seen. Being locked in the brig for days hadn't helped. No, being marooned on an uncharted desert island did not fit Candelario's plan at all.

Candelario knew it wasn't fair to shut Saif out of their world, but an entire kingdom depended on keeping Shiva's identity secret. No one could know where Emperor Chong Zhen's daughter was. No one, not even the pirate Candelario had grown to trust.

Smew was back and while he and Shiva shared the work of building the fire, Amadahy prepared the food for cooking.

45

"And just what of that beautiful steed?" Shiva inquired of the captain.

"Oh you know, conformation conundrums," he replied. "Typical for livestock in these parts. Base-narrow an' long pasterns. We can't have him goin' lame on us now, can we? Nay, I'll keep lookin'", Smew teased back and Shiva giggled. "How's yer fire comin' along, love?" Smew asked.

"It won't be long now, Capitán," She replied.

Shiva, however, was so hungry that she kept leaving the fire-tending to sit next to Amadahy. "Amadahy, look at that beautiful sunset!" Exclaimed Shiva, with all the sincerity she could muster. She may have said it because it was in fact beautiful, or she may have said it to get Amadahy to turn her head.

Amadahy did not seem to mind Shiva's light hearted deception. Everyone was hungry and as Shiva pointed at the sun with one hand, she quickly grabbed more food with the other.

47

Captain Smew skewered the bird with a stick and lay next to the fire to cook the meat. The searing heat nearly singed his eyebrows off. It was Amadahy's suggestion to sear the meat and keep the juices inside, *but not at the expense of me eyebrows*, Smew thought.

"Shiver me timbers—that be toasty!" he exclaimed, as he nearly dropped the feast into the flames. Shiva moved closer to offer assistance. So, Smew lay on his belly in the sand, holding the roasting sticks while Shiva held a piece of shipwrecked lumber to shield his face against the red hot glow.

Amadahy had wrapped the tubers she dug with leaves and mud but was using a long forked stick to carefully place them into the coals without needing to get too close.

"Best ye take care Amadahy," he warned, not wanting her to suffer the same fate he had. He knew she had learned much growing up with her mother and their Wampanoag tribe. She did still have her eyebrows after all.

Too slowly, and far too clumsily, everything was cooked to perfection. More than once the fowl dipped low in the fire and touched the burning sticks. *There be a bit more flame than I'd like, but we be too hungry to wait for that perfect bed o' coals,* Smew thought.

This only gonna add to its smoky flavor, Smew rationalized, looking to see if anyone noticed. If they did, they didn't say anything.

One of the skewer sticks even poked through the thoroughly cooked meat making it difficult to turn the bird and cook the other side. He had to stab it with his sword to keep it from slipping around. *Maybe next time we'll do it like Shiva suggested,* Smew sighed, *with a longer stick across the whole fire to turn the meat slowly, hmm.* Smew and his mates were hungry and the tantalizing aroma as the sizzling juices dripped onto the white-hot embers made Smew's mouth water in anticipation. He heard little Shiva's belly grumbling loudly as she licked her dry lips. *Poor thing,* he thought, *she must be starving.*

He had developed a definite fondness for the child over the years, and though he tried to hide those feelings, it broke his heart to see her suffer. She didn't know it but several times on board the ship he had given her his own rations. *Watching this lil' tadpole grow up these past few years, she be the closest thing to a daughter I probly ever gonna have,* he thought. He knew he loved her, though the word was not common in his vocabulary. Smew watched them all as they smiled in anticipation of the first fresh meat any of them had had in weeks. He was pleased that they would soon have full bellies.

Finally it was time for the 'Keep to the Code' door that they had found to be brought next to the fire. *Thar must be some shipwrecked pirates about,* Smew thought, when he first saw the board. He considered the potential ramifications of sharing the island with cutthroat privateers. *I reckon we gonna have to jump off that bridge when we get to it,* he decided.

"Somebody fetch that table so I don't drop the bird in the sand," Smew ordered. Shiva, who was already up, dropped the heat shield to grab the table from between Amadahy's legs. Smew winced from the rush of heat and he glared at Shiva for a micro-instant. Smew placed the hunk of slightly charred meat beside the other food on the makeshift table and the feast was ready to begin. "Wait," Smew said. "Somebody should say grace." He looked to Amadahy.

Amadahy looked to the stars, raised her hands palms open and facing each other and said something in Wampanoag, the tongue of her people. The other three looked at each other, shrugged their shoulders, smiled and said "Amen".

Amadahy tore a chunk of white bird meat from the breast and handed the first bite of fowl to the captain. "Capt'n Smew, you eat first," she said, out of respect.

He gladly bit into it as he said, "Hunger be the best sauce in the world." Smew quoted his favorite book, Don Quixote. He liked how one man would take upon himself such a mission. "Yarrr me hearties! What say ye we be fer eatin' this beast?" Grinning from ear to ear the four hungry pirates ate the roots and devoured the tasty flesh. It had that open fire, slightly burned taste with the skin charred to a certain crunchy texture.

"Cap'n, ye know that thin's could be worse," Candelario began. "Aye" he continued, "we could ha' been eaten by sharks, or dashed to bits by the surf. At least we be alive."

"Aye! And eatin' grub," Shiva chimed in, grinning ear to ear with mouth agape; showing the chewed up flesh for all to see. The four pirates erupted in hearty laughter.

Smew replied, "Yarr, me hearties, and that be better than a poke in th' eye with a sharp stick, surely!" They all laughed again, "Yo ho, ho!!" Lifting his bottle high in the air, Captain Smew caught Candelario's eyes as he leaned toward his mate. With furrowed brows and in pretend seriousness he began to speak. "Candy-boy, allow me to disambiguate sumpfin' here. Let the record state," the captain paused for effect then he grinned from ear to ear when he finished the sentence with, "that I be extra grog-filled we be buckos forever! Yarrr!" Just then he reached across and playfully punched Candelario in the arm. Unintentionally, his knuckles caught bone.

Candelario's expression changed in a heartbeat from a smile to a rigid, forced grimace. His mouth was still upturned in an almost smile but the eyes were strained and they watered. That punch missed flesh, hit solid bone, and it hurt. Smew could tell that Candelario didn't want it to show. Not willing to tolerate the awkward silence, Smew turned away and burst into laughter. When Smew's head was turned, Candelario quickly rubbed his arm.

To heighten the mood, Shiva asked, "Gunna ye be spinnin' us a yarn, Capitan? I heartily enjoy yer story tellin'." Amadahy smiled and nodded in agreement as Smew stood. Amadahy stoked the fire.

Candelario called out, "Aye, an' few there be unaware that our amazing, and humble, Captain Saif T. Smew needs little more than a nudge's worth of encouragement to get him to boast of his high seas adventures aboard his beloved Amazing Grace!"

What be the reason fer such hostilities? Smew wondered. *It were jus' a punch in the arm for cryin' all night.* As Smew's deep blue eyes reflected the flickering light of the campfire, he shrugged off the less than veiled jab at his character, as his face and hands began to emulate the energy and motion of the lively flames. And though Candelario's eyes burned holes through his thick skin, the thought to apologize was beyond the scope of Smew's talents. "'Twas in th' waters betwixt an' between Tattered Eye-patch Inlet and Davy Jones' Locker we were," he whispered. "I had in me sights a Spanish galleon, ridin' low in th' rum, an' rumored to be full o' Aztec silver 'n gold, 'n headed fer Spain. True in th' galleon's wake, wit' a strong wind in 'er sails, Gracie were gainin' on her prey, when without warnin', we lost all wind. Th' sails went slack, an' an eerie fog crept in o'er us like a dark smotherin' blanket. We were jolted to a sudden stop.

"It felt like we'd run aground, but then, quickly 'n violently th' ship were surrounded by churnin' spewin' sea water. In a flash, several monstrous tentacles lept from the sea all about us! It were a calamitous kettle o' fish fer sure. It was a kraken, a wicked giant of a sea monster whose evil habit 'twas to crush a ship, before pluckin' its crew from th' sea, one by one; aye, crunchin' its victims in that bone snappin' beak. Th' monster had us in its powerful grip, squeezin' me groanin' Gracie.

She were 'bout to break, like a bottle o' rum o'er a scurvy sea dog's head in a Tortuga pub, and spill her guts into the sea, all from the crushin' strength of them sinewy tentacles."

Although they had all heard Smew tell his stories before, the way he flailed his arms combined with his contorted facial expressions made him a joy to watch. Never was the account related exactly the same as before.

"While th' kraken was tryin' to break me ship's back, 'n drag her 'n th' crew to a dark 'n gloomy grave, I did what any," he paused for effect, and with a wry smile, shot a glance in the direction of his first mate, "'less than humble' pirate cap'n would do. I climbed the riggin' to th' top o' th' mizzenmast, I drew me sword, n I yelled, 'I gunna murder ye yet, ye putrid, rat spawned stick o' manure!' Or something to that effect.

Then I jumped into the kraken's most foul smelling, slimy, gullet! I, "amazing" Captain Saif T. Smew, cut 'n hacked 'n hacked 'n cut. I followed the thumpin' sound in me ears 'til I found th' beatin' heart o' that deplorable leviathan.

Slashin' wit' all me might, I severed th' boulder sized heart o' th' beastie in a pair, killin' th' behemoth instantly. Consequently, I were bathed in cold gooey blood.

Th' kraken released its grasp on me sighin' ship. Its gigantic tentacles, that a heartbeat hence, were slappin' men and canon like a horse swats flies, were now slitherin' across th' deck, an' slinkin' back to th' depths from whence they'd emerged, mere moments before.

Then I cut me way from th' belly o' that stinkin' monster, through its gurglin' gizzards, 'n fought me way up through its sinewy muscles, 'n slimy flesh, through the black water of night an' up to th' surface, 'n to the safety of me wounded ship 'n injured crew.

And who were tharr to pull me aboard but the most bestest first mate I could ever ask for?!" He stuck out his hand to Candelario, who had already forgiven him for the punch of earlier, and he took his hand.

A wry grin crept onto Smew's face and he exploded in high-spirited laughter, "Yo, ho, ho, ho, ho, ha, ha!! It gunna take more than one lone kraken to take below me beloved Gracie!" Candelario, Shiva and Amadahy laughed with delight.

While they laughed, Smew took a moment to glance toward the darkening horizon, and the sea. *Treacherous deeds allowed evil men to strip me of me vessel. Men, too superstitious to allow a woman on a ship, and believin' everything bad that happened was the result*, he thought.

"Tell us another, Capitán," Shiva pleaded. "Tell us about the biggest treasure in the world!"

"Oh, so ye want to hear 'bout Avery's Folly do ye now?" inquired the captain. "Very well then, I gunna start by saying that Cap'n Avery, Henry Avery, were both the luckiest an' the unluckiest scurvy sea dog pirate on the seven seas.

As ye know, Avery lived about a hundred years hence. How he came to be a pirate aren't very important to this story, but suffice it to say he weren't always a corsair. Nay, so one day Avery and his crew, who were accompanied by two quick an' maneuverable sloops, were lookin' to plunder a merchant class vessel when they jus' happened upon a large slowish veshel, slowish veshel, vessssel. Easy fer me to say," he joked.

"Before," Shiva asserted.

"What? Before what?" Smew inquired.

"You said hence, but I think you meant 'before' or 'ago'."

"Aye, before then. Before what?"

"Mi Capitán! You said Avery lived 100 years hence."

"Aye, that's what I said. Why? What did you "thunk" I said?"

"But hence means in the future, so he lived before."

"Twaddle speak and balderdash! You know what I meant," said Smew as he rolled his eyes and smiled, a little embarrassed that he misused a word.

"And thunk is not a real word. Ha...ha...ha," she laughed sarcastically, pausing between each 'ha'. "So what happened next?" Shiva asked.

"How did you get so smart, then?"

"You know Candelario makes me read."

"It were a rhetorical question, smarty breeches, but mighty good for Candelario," Smew replied.

He continued, "As Avery approached the vessel, he commanded the English colors to be lowered and the Jolly Roger to be hoisted. The merchants had thought Avery's ships were English so they allowed them alongside. By the time they discovered the ruse it were too late. The surrounded ship saw she were 'bout to be attacked by pirates of the surroundin' ships, so she dropped her sails. To avoid takin' cannon fire from all sides, surely, and to avoid any harm to their oh-so-precious cargo." Smew stopped to take a sip.

"What happened then? What precious cargo?" Shiva asked, on the edge of her log. Ignoring her for the moment to add suspense, Smew reached over, grabbed some firewood and built the fire up a bit. He squatted next to the fire, used the tip of his cutlass to move some half burned sticks toward the center of the fire pit then stared into the flames to await Shiva's next question.

Predictably, and with wide curious eyes, Shiva asked again, "Pero mi capitán, What precious cargo?"

Smew smiled and stood again. "Being somewhat new to the art of piracy and in his haste, what Avery

failed to realize," the captain continued, "Was that the ship, wot he were plunderin', belonged to the daughter of the most powerful emperor to inhabit the earth, at the time. Akbar the Great was the greatest emperor the Mughal Empire had ever known. Even the English Empire feared what his armies could do to their settlements in India."

"Anywho, it was Akbar the Great's daughter who commanded that vessel, as she was on her voyage to Mecca, the holy city of Islam. She was making her haj, ye know, her holy pilgrimage, and so she were accompanied by most of her royal court and the most amazing treasure anyone had ever laid his eyes upon. There were chests of gold and precious gems and especially diamonds. Akbar the Great had many diamond mines ye know."

"What I wouldn't do for half of that treasure," Candelario blurted out.

"Aye, as would I Candy-boy," agreed Captain Smew. Again baiting Shiva, he asked, "Now, who remembers? Wherrrre... was I?"

"A princess with chests of diamonds and gold," replied Shiva to his rhetorical question. Smew laughed.

"Aye, little tadpole. Diamonds and gold, lots and lots o' diamonds and gold," Smew responded.

"And a princess, don't forget about the princess," Shiva reminded, her eyes casting unconsciously in Candelario's direction for an instant.

Smew smiled in response. "So Avery's men boarded the princess's ship with nary a life lost on either side. In fact, there were very few shots that were even fired. The princess's guard never thought anyone so foolish to steal from the Mughal Emperor nor kidnap his daughter so they were rather unprepared for such an occasion.

To engage in a skirmish would undoubtedly put the princess in harm's way, so they protected her as best they could by surrounding her."

For the first time Amadahy spoke, "They kidnap the father's daughter?"

"Aye, Amadahy." Until now, Smew had not considered the affect this story would have on someone who had also been taken from her family.

"So while the treasure and the princess were bein' transferred to Avery's vessel, Avery were curious as to why this one girl were bein' surrounded by armed guards. In fact, from the safety of his own ship, Avery saw that it were the girl who commanded those guards.

At first, Avery thought to hold her for ransom, as if the chests of booty plundered already weren't enough. It is not known how but just as Avery's ships were pulling away from the plundered Mughal ship, somehow Avery discovered that the princess were the daughter of the infamous Akbar the Great. Everyone that was anyone had heard o' the power of Akbar the Great and Avery, not being the bravest of souls, but to his credit, having sufficient intelligence to know when to back down, decided to put the princess back aboard her own ship.

When the emperor heard what had happened, that an Englishman had stolen his treasure and tried to kidnap his daughter, he was furious, as mad as Davy Jones gettin' hornswoggled into extra years o' service, or somethin' along those lines, as one might well imagine.

Akbar the Great sent a message to England in response, threatenin' to destroy every English settlement in India if the plunderin' English thief were not found and delivered to him within a fortnight's time. England promised to deliver but Avery were a sneaky scalawag and not wantin' to be found, he weren't. At first he escaped to America then to Ireland. Little by little he divvied up a portion of the treasure amongst the crew aboard his vessel, the Duke. But not before cheating the crews of the two sloops out of all of it. But that be another story for another campfire, yarrr!

"So why is Avery the unluckiest pirate ever?" Shiva inquired in earnest. "You said he were the unluckiest sea dog. So far he sounds pretty lucky to me," Shiva mused.

Chapter Four
Avery's Curse

An' to make matters even more worse, much, more worser in fact, the angry emperor, whose vengeance had gone unsatisfied, up to this point, demanded justice by any means necessary. And, since Avery could not be found...

Oh my, lookey tharr. It be getting' late. What say ye we continue this another time?"

"Noooooooo!!!" replied Shiva, Candelario, and Amadahy in unison. "Yo, ho, ho, ho," laughed Captain Smew.

"Alright then," he continued, but this time he spoke in a raspy whisper, as if he were telling a ghost story. "Akbar the Great had many forces at his command. Among them, evil sorcerers and not less than a few wizards. He commanded his most powerful sorceress, Uma Ayn el Hasuud, to seek out and curse Captain Henry Avery for the wicked acts he had committed. Uma Ayn el Hasuud cursed Avery that he would be forever trapped inside his skull. He could speak but it would be in an old woman's voice. Other things went along with it but no man alive be knowin' the extent o' the curse. Uma Ayn cursed him that he were gonna be drawn to the palace of Akbar the Great, where he'd be deftly removed from his body. After that, Akbar commanded that Avery's head be placed in a box an' buried on an uncharted island, never to be found.

But, Avast, to give Avery one miniscule chance at redemption, an enchanted map leadin' to the box would be placed in a cursed bottle. They say th' bottle circles that unknown island an' comes to shore only once... every ten years. If some unfortunate soul happens upon the bottle, and weren't careful, he would be cursed as well."

"What were the curse, Capitan? What would happen?" Shiva asked, curiosity always driving her to want to know more.

"Alas, me fair Shiva, no one alive knows the curse wot may befall the discoverer of said bottle. However, it be told that Avery will be compelled to guide the one with the map to the greatest treasure imaginable. An everlasting treasure! The real truth is that it were most likely a made up bedtime story to get little someday pirates to go to sleep! Ha ha ha! Yarrr me hearties!! Enough stories for now!" Bellowed the captain.

All of a sudden, Smew drew his sword and pointed it directly at Candelario. "Candelario, ye lice infested, mermaid marryin', skirt wearin' cargo thievin' scabby sea bass, I challenge ye to a duel. Do ye accept this challenge?"

"There be no place I'd rather be, an' nothing I'd rather do than to fight and kill a grog snarfin' parrot stranglin' bilge rat like yerself, Cap'n Saif T. Smew," Candelario replied as he jumped to his feet weapon already in hand. They had played this game before and it meant Captain Smew wanted to practice swordsmanship. The idea of the game was to taunt the opponent with piratical insults then follow up with swordplay. Smew usually won the insult part, Candelario always won the swordplay.

Following suit Shiva challenged Amadahy, and being careful to not step in the fire, the four of them honed skills that had previously, and might again, save their lives.

With a sword Shiva was quick and agile. As such, she was able to hold her own against many, which seemed to please Candelario, who saw to it that Shiva practiced daily. Amadahy was deadly with a knife, both in close and at range. When forced to fight she used her sword and knife in synchronized harmony, but it was well known that she much preferred cooking to fighting.

After clear victors had been established, Smew encouraged Caldelario, "Candy-boy, ye know what they say, 'where there be music, there can be no evil'. What say ye lead us in a sea shanty?"

Candelario was always breaking out in song anyway, so he began to lead the merry pirates in an upbeat shanty. A shanty normally reserved for hauling in the anchor rode. They all knew it well.

After the first chorus, Smew grabbed Amadahy and began jumping around the fire. It was his version of dancing but Shiva giggled because she thought it looked funny. Shiva began an artful interpretation, which was far more elegant than what the captain was doing.

When she was young, Amadahy learned the ways of her mother's tribe, the Mashpee tribe, and so she began a dance of gratitude to honor her Wampanoag Nation.

For a while, it seemed as if they had nearly forgotten they were marooned and that their ship had been stolen. *We be just making the best of a bad situation. And why not? Who really knows how long we gonna be stuck here?* Smew thought.

Eventually they sat back down, stoked the fire and watched the firebrands sail upward to disappear into the murky night sky. One by one, when their eyes grew heavy, they slipped into an exhausted slumber, accompanied by only the shifting smoke and the intermittent crackle of the fire's dying embers.

To help him fall asleep, Smew counted gold doubloons falling into a wooden chest. Clink, clink, clink. *What great adventures will befall us on the morrow*, he thought as he embarked on yet another journey to slumber land.

Chapter Five
Barnacles and Blood

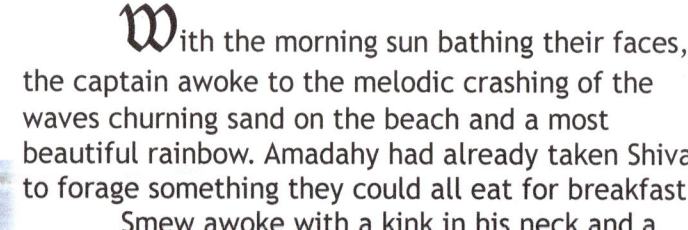

With the morning sun bathing their faces, the captain awoke to the melodic crashing of the waves churning sand on the beach and a most beautiful rainbow. Amadahy had already taken Shiva to forage something they could all eat for breakfast.

Smew awoke with a kink in his neck and a sore hip from the harder sleeping surface than he was used to in his captain's quarters. While he was stretching his neck to the left and to the right, something moving down by the water caught his attention.

Candy-boy, look over yonder!" Captain Smew motioned toward something caught in the rocks at the water's edge. Candelario didn't move. This time he nudged his first mate and said, "Candelario, Show a leg. What say ye go and fetch yon object, so we can spy wit' our eye what it contains, if anythin'. Maybe tharr be rum!" When the captain said "Candelario" instead of "Candy-boy" that usually meant it was more of an order than a suggestion.

Candelario was curious by nature, so, still groggy from just waking up, he hastened to get to his feet. The ever seasoned warrior was seldom more than arms length from his sword. He grabbed his cutlass, but he didn't want to get his boots wet again, so, bare footed, Candelario darted through the sand and rocks to grab the object before it was reclaimed by the sea.

Candelario looked surprised when he peered through the barnacle encrusted glass. It seemed to be a piece of parchment that was rolled up inside the decrepit bottle. The cork proved to be wedged in tightly. The entire thing was mostly wrapped in leather.

I wonder if this be a treasure map or a message from a lover, wondered Candelario. Won't this be great to share with me mates, if it really is a treasure map? He laughed incredulously. With his left hand Candelario gripped the neck of the bottle tightly.

With his right he attempted to free the cork from the bottle's orifice. It wouldn't budge. He tried harder. "Ouch!" He yelped out loud, teeth gritted together in anger. It was then that he cut his thumb on one of the barnacles. In that instant, the adrenaline rush ripped the air from his chest. When he caught his breath, Candelario was focused on one thing and one thing only. Treasure.

Are the stories of the Cursed Skull Treasure really true? Candelario wondered. *If this bottle be the one, then we be, nay, belay that. I be one lucky pirate indeed. This could be jus' the treasure I need to buy an army, become emperor and return to my beautiful homeland. If this be a map to a treasure, I gunna be having it all to me lonesome*, Candelario thought. The desire to have the treasure and not share it, was all-consuming. It felt like a fire had ignited within Candelario's bosom; worldly riches were all the pirate craved. The ravenous desire to get what was at the other end of the map was his only goal. Nothing else mattered. Not friendship, not loyalty, nothing. Everything he had done up to this point was to serve Emperor Chong Zhen, Shiva, and Smew. *What a waste of my life*, Candelario thought. This sudden greed was not something he was familiar with. Candelario sat and tried to remove the parchment from its container.

After Smew finished donning his dry boots and belts, he looked and noticed something peculiar about Candelario's demeanor. *Candy-boy still be tryin' to get that tharr cork from that bottle, and he looks angry,* he thought. Smew asked, "What did ye find tharr? Candy-boy, what ye be seein' in that tharr bottle that seems to have ye so perplexed, matey?" Candelario didn't acknowledge that he had even heard the captain. *That were a wee bit strange. Perhaps he didn't hear me,* Smew thought. "Avast Candy-boy," Smew yelled, louder, to get his mate's attention, but again, he was ignored.

Richard W. Dyer

As a pirate feverishly obsessed, opening the bottle seemed to be the only thing on Candelario's mind. Curious, Smew began to close the distance between them. When he got closer he saw a bottle covered in barnacles poorly wrapped in leather and tied with a black cord. That image summoned memories of childhood fables. *Many a pirate died searching for that legendary fortune*, Smew thought. *Could tis be our lucky day?* Instinctively, he reached for the bottle.

79

To avoid Smew's reach, Candelario twisted away. When he did the jagged edge of a dead barnacle cut Smew's palm. Smew winced from the pain in his hand. He had been cut while scraping barnacles many times but this was different. It felt like a jellyfish sting with a kick to the chest for good measure.

He made a second, more fervent effort and managed to grab hold of the bottle, but Candelario held tight. "Candelario! Belay this nonsense and be smart about it! I be needin' to spy wit' me own eye," demanded Smew, but he could feel Candelario pull even harder. Smew knew he was stronger and figured he would wrest the bottle from his first mate's grip through the power of sheer force. Imagining an everlasting treasure, the most ravenous, covetous sensation swept over them both as each struggled for sole possession of the map that would lead them to riches beyond their wildest dreams.

81

By this time Candelario had loosed the cork. With one hand on the cork and the other on the bottle Candelario released the bottle which Smew held firmly with both hands. Unbeknownst to the captain, the cork had a string attached which Candelario could see was tied around the parchment. When he released the bottle with his right hand, in his left he retained the cork and the string. The parchment came flying out in one direction while Smew fell to his back in the opposite direction, still clutching the bottle.

Candelario quickly opened the parchment to discover that it was indeed a map.

Smew jumped to his feet and managed to get both hands on the map, but Candelario deftly pivoted his feet, hip threw the captain and tossed him like a rag doll. Never releasing his grip, the nimble Smew returned to his feet. "I demand that ye give me that map, now! I be captain, wot makes the map mine!" Captain Smew commanded, as he leapt to his feet.

"If ye want it ye will have to take it over me rottin' corpse," retorted the first mate.

"I care not a fiddlestick that ye'd rather die, ye mutinous, thievin' scoundrel," replied Smew as he jumped forward just in time to grab hold of the corner of the map. Both pirates wrestled for possession of it and in the struggle the map was torn.

The captain barely had time to draw his sword from his scabbard in response to Candelario's aijutsu attack. Smew knew he could not best the younger, quicker swordsman with his first mate's weapon of preference. Candelario snarled at him, "Ye don't be wantin' to cross blades wit' me, cap'n, lest ye want me to see ye to Davy Jones!"

The two pirates seemed to have utterly forgotten that moments ago they were best mates. Greed spawned anger, which erupted into wild intemperate rage.

The curse seemed to magnify emotions normally kept at bay by a bridled humanity.

The two tenacious pirates battled, determined to secure both halves of the map, Candelario by supremacy with the sword and Smew by trickery, but Candelario's skill clearly gave a distinct advantage. At one point, Smew was on his back against some rocks with Candelario bearing down.

A thrust kick to the chest gave the captain the space he needed to scale the rocks. Fearing for his life, Smew thought, *Candy-boy has the wind o' me! I best make meself scarce while I still have me head!* He threw a fistful of sand at Candelario's face and headed for the open beach.

89

Smew took advantage of
Candelario's barefootedness
and scampered up some rocks.

Smew's Greed

92

When he bent over to recover his tricorn Candelario was upon him in an instant!

Chapter Six
Swallowed Whole

"Do you think they're awake yet?" Shiva asked.

"Ha ha, Father Sun awake plenty. Make hard for Capt'n Smew to sleep, so he probably awake by now and runnin' up and down the beach, enjoying himself plenty," Amadahy replied.

"This should be enough for us four," said Amadahy. Amadahy was taller so she picked while Shiva held her sash open to hold the hard fruit.

Livid with a blinding rage, the relentlessly strong-willed Candelario chased the wily captain zigging and zagging down the beach. Candelario's dogged pursuit was skillful and strategic. With each stroke of his cutlass he deftly maneuvered the captain closer to defeat and closer...

...to the edge of the rock face.

With a 20 foot drop to violent waves, wicked currents, and jagged rocks, getting forced over the ledge was something Smew wanted to avoid, if at all possible. Spending much of his time with his feet pointing away from his opponent, in escape mode, was opening him up for all kinds of attacks from behind. *Damn his fighting skills*, Smew's mind raced.

Smew's Greed

Richard W. Dyer

He was so focused on not getting skewered, that he barely noticed the gaping pit in his path. *Candelario be slowed down a bit fer not havin' boots*, Smew thought.

"It's apparent by all yer pussy-footin' around that yer not gonna be winnin' this fight, mate," Smew told his adversary. He noticed the sharpness of the sea worn rocks and was grateful for the slight advantage they afforded.

Backed against the edge with nowhere left to go Smew lept to an archway above a large pit filled with violently churning water. Without boots, Candelario could pursue no further on the razor sharp rocks.

    Although he was clear of Candelario's slashing cutlass, Smew knew he had been backed into a corner. Of course that was Candelario's intention, so he sat down to wait the captain out. "Eventually yer gonna have to come back this way and when you do, I'll get me map, Candelario said. He was the most patient combatant Smew had ever met.

Smew's Greed

Out of sheer frustration, as not having anything else to do, the captain began to taunt Candelario, knowing he wouldn't attempt the arch crossing in stocking feet. "Look at wot I got!" Smew smirked. "You got that right, mate! I got yer precious little map and I'm gonna keep it! If you want it yer gonna have to come get it. What's that ye say? No boots? Awww. Wot an ill prepared pirate ye arrr! Wot kind o' pirate leaves camp wot not wearin' any boots? Yo ho ho ho! Ye don't even deserve this map fer bein' so short sighted.

"Dance around all you want ye pompous parrot lovin' poor excuse for a ship's captain. We wouldn't even be here if it weren't fer you. Incidentally, as ye know, I can wait here fer days."

Smew knew Candelario was right. *He will do that meditation thing and not even sleep,* Smew thought. *He's not givin' me much options here, me thinks.* He began to descend to the center of the archway.

"Cap'n Smew, ye bilge sucking, ballast pig, if ye don' bring me map back," over the crashing waves Smew heard Candelario yelling, "I'll cleave ye to th' brisket and run ye through wit' me blade! It be me map after all, since I got to it first!"

But Candelario's angry shouts were in vain. Because halfway through Candelario's rant, Smew sheathed his sword, stuffed his map inside his sash, and held onto his precious tricorn.

He shot Candelario a come and get me smirk. For good measure, he quoted Don Quixote once again and said, "Until death, it is all life." With that, Captain Smew took one giant step and disappeared from view into the churning, water-filled pit below.

Candelario slowly pushed himself to his feet. Using his sword as a cane, he walked carefully back across the sharp volcanic rock to the softer sand where a more thorough study of the torn section of parchment could be performed without jagged sea worn rocks jabbing into the soles of his bloody bare feet.

Chapter Seven
Godly Sorrow

ℬack in camp, Amadahy and Shiva were just arriving. Shiva was carrying some fruit and other edible plants that she and Amadahy had found. Not one to overlook the details, Amadahy saw blood on the bottle she was holding. *I wonder if Capt'n Smew were injured*, she thought.

"Where be Capt'n Smew?" Amadahy asked.

Smew's Greed

Uncharacteristically, Candelario mocked Amadahy's pronunciation, "Capt'n Smew, he be lost or drowned by now. An' better off we be for it," he replied with no explanation for his mean spirited lack of concern.

Confused and incredulous, Amadahy thought, *Candelario's face say angry, not sad, but if Capt'n Smew be drowned, why Candelario so angry*

"But Candelario, we are to believe that out of nowhere the captain tried to kill ye for a treasure map? Nay, balderdash! It makes no sense at all." Shiva looked to Amadahy for support.

"Ye be callin' me a liar, whelp?" Candelario challenged young Shiva, who immediately backed down when she saw the contorted and irate expression of hatred on the first mate's face.

Amadahy had only seen Candelario look like that in battle. She thought how the warrior looked possessed of a demon spirit.

After a few agonizingly long seconds Shiva continued her protest, but with more finesse. "Surely the captain will *cool off* and come back to camp." Shiva put stress on the words 'cool off' probably hoping Candelario would get the hint, Amadahy thought. Candelario is the one that needs to cool off, Amadahy thought. She dared not say it out loud. Candelario merely grunted her disapproval.

118

Amadahy wasn't buying any of Candelario's lies, and she could tell that Shiva wasn't buying into them either, but Amadahy knew better than to challenge the seasoned warrior. Although Amadahy did not fully understand the dynamics between Candelario and Shiva, Amadahy never felt it was her place to question the status quo or make waves. She was only the ship's cook, after all, and fairly low on the totem pole. *Candelario could have me flogged with a cat-o-nine tails on a whim. At least that's how it was on the Duke where Amadahy were a galley slave, and before Capt'n Smew rescue me from that life*, Amadahy thought.

Many of her people, the Wampanoag Nation, were made slaves on ships and for plantations in the West Indies. How her proud people had gone from rescuing the Pilgrims that first winter to slavery was beside her. They had developed a written language from their language in order to make deals for land with the whites, who were flooding her land, but the whites failed to honor those agreements. She wondered how her people were.

Amadahy wondered as these two pirates dug in the earth for yellow metal and other treasure. Sure it was pretty, but she failed to comprehend the strangle hold that gold could have on certain greedy individuals. Most of all she wondered how Candelario could search for treasure when, if what Candelario said was true, Captain Smew's life was in danger. Anyway, she knew her place on this crew and was grateful for it. No sense rocking the boat now. No, she did her job and she stayed out of trouble.

Amadahy's concern heightened when Candelario mentioned the captain's fate. "Cap'n Smew fell into a pit o' water but I were unable to save him because of the sharp rocks," Candelario insisted rather unconvincingly. Come on girls! Let us start to dig fer buried treasure. With the map and some luck perhaps we'll strike it rich," Candelario said.

Amadahy was not interested in material wealth. It had never held much allure for her. Especially when the captain could need her help. "Where be this pit?" Amadahy inquired. Without looking up, Candelario pointed down the beach. With a slight nod and a wink to Shiva, but without speaking a word, Amadahy dropped the bottle and walked off in the direction Candelario had indicated.

The waves breaking along the beach were as large today as they had been yesterday when they swam through them. In search of the man whom she esteemed as her rescuer, Amadahy hoped that perhaps she could return the favor.

Smew's Greed

The thirst that drove Candelario to obtain the treasure was unquenchable. He hurriedly began putting on his boots and effects. "Shiva, we gunna be lookin' fer treasure now so put down those roots," Candelario demanded, referring to the fruit Shiva still held in her arms.

"Shouldn't we go...help Amadahy...find the captain?" Shiva asked in halted disbelief.

"Smew can take care o' himself. Now we gunna search for treasure," Candelario replied resolutely.

"Candelario, what's the matter? Are ye angry with me?" Shiva, who had never seen Candelario act like this toward her, was confused.

"No Shiva," I'm not upset with you, but it's urgent we find the treasure, NOW!" Candelario's voice elevated significantly, growling the end of his sentence. "Besides, we can use this treasure to get yer kingdom back and rescue yer father. Don't you wish for this, princess?"

"I thought you told me never to mention that and besides, I jus' don't see the urgency," Shiva protested. "I mean, we're not going anywhere anytime soon, are we? Unless you know something I do not."

"No, probably not, but just in case," Candelario replied tersely. Candelario was clearly growing agitated with the questions. All of this talking was not helping to find the treasure. His voice was tense and many of the words spoken were pronounced through gritted teeth and with brow furrowed.

Just then Shiva spotted the brown rolled up parchment poking out from inside Candelario's sash. Shiva asked, "Is that a map? A treasure map? Was it in that bottle? Can I see it? Ye gunna let me see it Candelario, aren'tcha?" But Candelario ignored her completely and went back to studying the section of map in her hand.

Shiva groped desperately for some semblance of order to the buzzing chaos that swarmed in her head. Her squinting intensified. Her breathing swallowed. Fissured eyes an opening to a confused mind. Her own brow mirrored Candelario's. *This makes not one iota of sense*, she thought. Her insatiable curiosity could not let it go. "But, shouldn't...we...?"

Candelario screamed, "Shiva! Enough with the questions!"

A single droplet of spittle catapulted through the air and lit upon Shiva's face. With her sleeve Shiva wiped her cheek. The creases deepened between Candelario's furrowed brow, which itself was bookended by dark narrow slits. Candelario's face was red in the cheeks. His nostrils flared making his nose wider than normal. His reddish lips snarled to reveal too much gum and teeth. He inhaled deeply and with as much control as humanly possible, under the circumstances, he spoke through gritted teeth, "Look, child. Just. Do." Another calming breath, "As. You. Are. Told. Or else!" Each word came out as a separate veiled admonishment. The "or else" came out as a snarl. It was a threat for sure. A scary one. One Shiva had no intention of putting to the test.

Be sure to keep a weather eye out for
the rest of the adventure in:

Seven Deadly Sins of a Pirate:
Smew's Greed: Part II

Remember, Younger pirates can check

Smew's Nook

on YouTube for popular pirate stories read by Captain Smew.

More videos coming soon!

https://www.youtube.com/watch?v=cfUguz6r78I

Coming soon
Free Audio Book Version of Smew's Greed:
Author Web page:
https://www.RichardWDyer.com

Acknowledgements

The creation of this work has only been possible through the support and help of family and friends. First and foremost I wish to express my gratitude to Tracy Shaffner for being the spark to ignite the tinder of the fire that has become this project. The words, "We should make a picture book," still ring in my ears. Mahalo my friend.

To those friends along the way who have lent an encouraging word, you have my undying gratitude. This road has been long and replete with obstacles. Please know that without your friendly encouraging words, the arduous path is easier left to the lion hearted. Mahalo.

Becca, you brought a maturity and sanity to the set that was most helpful. Your advice on matters technical was always welcome. I am grateful for your enduring friendship and ever willingness to assist. Mahalo.

Candice, you have always believed in me and what we are doing. Your heart is so big and full of love that it spills out into your smile, which although not always wanted during the more serious scenes, was always enjoyed and appreciated. Your 'love fills the universe' attitude is a blessing, especially when times are trying. Mahalo.

Sujin, those many road trips to photo shoots of us bouncing crazy imaginitive ideas around, were, in part, fuel to feed my imagination. Without imagination, creativity is dead, so for that I thank you. Mahalo.

To my children, Chelsea, Ricky, Becky, and Annie, and my wife, Mayville, you always have my back. The love and support you have shown me throughout this process is much appreciated. You've always believed in me and I am humbled. Everything I do is for you. You are the end of my rainbow.

Glossary of Piratese

Alas: An expression of grief, concern or pity.

Avast ye: Stop, and check this out!

Betwixt and between: in a midway position; so-so; neither one thing nor the other.

Blimey: Exhortation of surprise.

Blow me down!: Expression of shock or disbelief.

Boatswain (pronounced bosun): an officer in charge of rigging, cables, anchors, etc.

Booty: Treasure.

Bucko: Short for buccaneer or pirate. Sometimes used as "friends".

Chanty: Also spelled Shantey or Chantey. Song originally sung by sailors to keep their rhythm as they worked. Originates from the
French 'chanter' which means to sing.

Cleave him to the brisket: To cut across the chest, from one shoulder to the lower abdomen.

Crow's Nest: A small platform atop the mast where the lookout stands.

Cutlass: Short, heavy, curve-bladed sword used by pirates in close quarters.

Davy Jones' Locker: Fabled, mythical place at the bottom of the ocean, where the evil spirit of Davy Jones
brings sailors and pirates to die.

Galleon: A sailing ship (especially by Spain) from the 15th through the 17th centuries, used originally as a warship,
and later for trade because they are fast and carry much cargo.

Grog-filled: Grog is rum, usually mixed with water and lemon juice to ward off scurvy. 'Grog-filled' means happy.

Hang the jib: To pout or frown.

Hearties: Friends.

Heave-Ho: Give it some muscle and push it.

Hornswoggle: To defraud or cheat out of money or belongings.

Huli-huli chicken: Hawaii's version of barbecued chicken, cooked rotisserie style and flavored with a blend of spices.

Jot and Tittle: modicum, little bit

Glossary of Piratese

Kraken: A common ocean-dwelling monster of purported proportions that would allow it to attack a large ocean

going vessel and drag her to the sea. Most probably a mythical creature based on exaggerated sightings of

giant squid.

Left to feed the fish: Left to die.

Marooned: Put ashore and abandoned on a desolate island or coast, often with food so that the one doing the marooning could not

later be accused of murdering the one being marooned.

Mate/Matey: Friend, shipmate.

Nary: Not one.

Rum: Pirate's traditional alcoholic beverage. The ocean may also be referred to as rum.

Salt/Salty: An old, experienced sailor.

Savvy?: Do you understand, and do you agree?

Scallywag: A mild insult, akin to rapscallion or rogue.

Scurvy: A disease caused by vitamin C deficiency that once plagued sailors, pirates, and others on long voyages without proper diet.

Sea Dog: old pirate or sailor.

See a man about a horse: urinate

Shiver me Timbers!: Comparable to "Oh my gosh!" as an exclamation of surprise.

Sloop: Often the vessel of preference for pirates because of their speed.

Spoils: Spoils of war, that which is plundered from another.

Tricorn hat: a cocked hat with the brim turned up to form three points or hornlike projections.

Walk the plank: punishment in which a person walks off a board jutting over the side of the ship while at sea. The consequence is

drowning and a visit to Davy Jones' Locker.

Wee bit: little bit; small amount.